Balloon Ride

For Douglas

ACKNOWLEDGMENTS

The author wishes to thank the following people for their help: Firefly's pilot and crew: Joy Carbone, Elaine Walker, Betty Walsh, and Megan Walsh. Also Brian Asack, Barbara Bates, Georg Brewer, Chuck Daly, The Reverend N. Dean Evans, Alison Kelley, Mark Kissling, Richard P. Kughn, Lakeside Writers for Young People, Carol Mayer, Celeste Meola, Christopher Mott, Cecilia Palestini, Photo-Video of Yardley, Frank Pronesti, The Reverend Nancy M. Stroh, Amy Shields, Trenton Public Library, Nancy van Laan, Yardley-Makefield Branch of the Bucks County Free Library.

First published in the United States of America in 1991 by Walker Publishing Company, Inc.

Published simultaneously in Canada by Thomas Allen & Son Canada, Limited, Markham, Ontario.

Library of Congress Cataloging-in-Publication Data
Mott, Evelyn Clarke.
Balloon ride / text and photographs by Evelyn Clarke Mott.
p. cm.
Summary: Megan goes for a ride in a hot-air balloon and learns all the details of how one operates them.
ISBN 0-8027-8124-1 (trade). —ISBN 0-8027-8126-8 (rein.)
[1. Hot air balloons—Fiction. 2. Balloon ascensions—Fiction.]
I. Title.
PZ7.M8572Bal 1991
[E]—dc20 91-9881
CIP
AC

PRINTED IN HONG KONG

2 4 6 8 10 9 7 5 3 1

Balloon Ride

EVELYN CLARKE MOTT

Walker and Company
New York

Early in the morning, Megan runs outside. The sky is blue and a gentle breeze blows against her face.

"*Hooray!*" she shouts. "It's a perfect day to ride in a hot-air balloon."

Megan laughs with excitement as she races toward the launch field. The first person she meets is Joy, the pilot.

"Will you show me your balloon?" Megan asks.

"I'll be glad to," Joy replies. "Come with me. I'll show you how we get the balloon ready to fly."

"What's that on the ground?" Megan asks. "It looks like a long snake."

Joy laughs. "It looks funny, doesn't it? That's our balloon. We call it Firefly."

Megan and Joy watch two women unroll the big balloon across the field.

"Elaine and Betty are my ground crew," Joy says. "First, they help get Firefly ready for flight. Then, when we're up in the air, Elaine and Betty follow us in the van to help us land."

"Can I help, too, Joy?"

"Sure, Megan. This is the basket we will stand in. It's called a gondola. You can help me hook the cables to the balloon and gondola."

"Wow!" Megan exclaims. "There are a lot of cables."

"Yes." Joy smiles. "They keep the balloon and the gondola together."

Elaine and Joy hold open the mouth of the balloon, and Betty starts a large fan. WHIRRRRRRRR! The air blows into the balloon. Firefly begins to take shape.

"What are you doing?" Megan asks.

"We're filling the balloon with cold air."

"*Cold* air!" Megan exclaims. "But I thought Firefly was a hot-air balloon."

"It is," Joy says. "After Firefly is filled with cold air, we heat the air with a flame."

"Before we do that, we must make sure the inside of the balloon is safe."

Megan and Joy walk inside Firefly and look it over carefully. Megan feels as if she is walking inside a big tent.

"The balloon is in good shape, no rips or tears," Joy says. "It's time to heat the air inside of it."

Joy lights the gas burner above the gondola.
"Hold your ears, Megan!"

She opens the blast valve and shoots quick blasts
of flame into the balloon. The burner sounds like a
thousand roaring lions. RRRRROAR! RRRRROAR!
RRRRROAR! RRRRROAR!

With each blast, the air inside the balloon gets warmer. Elaine and Betty hold Firefly down as it starts to rise.

"What makes Firefly fly?" Megan asks.

"Hot air," answers Joy. "Hot air weighs less than cold air. So, when the air in Firefly is heated, the balloon goes up into the sky."

Joy makes a last check of the instruments, the burners, the gas tanks, and the lines. She shouts, *"All aboard!"*

Joy helps Megan into the gondola and then turns the burner on for a long time. RRRRRRRRRROAR!

Firefly gently takes off into the open sky.
"Hooray!" Megan yells. "Here we go!"

Firefly starts out low . . .

RRRRROAR!

. . . and then goes higher.

The balloon drifts across the sky.

Megan sees treetops and fields, horses and farms, a skydiver, and Firefly's shadow.

M̲egan and Joy smile when a bird flies underneath them.

Megan asks, "Where are we going?"

"Wherever the wind takes us," Joy answers. "Balloons can't be steered the way cars or airplanes can. I can only control how high or low we fly."

"But I don't feel any wind," Megan says.

"That's right," Joy says. "Since we're traveling with the wind, we don't feel the wind at all."

"Look, Megan. This is a compass. It tells us the direction we're traveling in. The wind is taking us to the north."

"The altimeter measures how high we are. Firefly is one thousand feet up."

Megan looks up into the balloon.
"It's so pretty," she says. "It looks like the quilt my grandma made me—only *bigger!*"

Joy turns off the burner and waits for the air inside the balloon to cool a little. Firefly starts to come down slowly.

"Let's go treetopping!" Joy lowers Firefly until its gondola scrapes the treetops.

Megan reaches out and grabs a fistful of leaves from a tall tree. "This is fun!" she shouts.

Joy gets in touch with Elaine by radio. "Can you see Firefly?" she asks.

"Yes, Joy. We're right with you."

"Good," Joy says. "There's an open field ahead of me that would be a great place to land. Could you get the owner's permission?"

A few minutes later, Elaine radios Joy, "Permission granted." Joy opens the release vent. Hot air slowly escapes from the balloon. Firefly drifts lower and lower toward the ground. THUMP! BUMP! Firefly lands.

Joy tugs the rip cord. The top of the balloon opens up and Firefly sighs as the hot air rushes out.

"Yea!" Megan cheers as she steps from the gondola.

Joy presents Megan with a Certificate of Ballooning Excellence. "Congratulations!" Joy says. "You did a great job."

Megan smiles widely and gives Joy a hug.

"Would you help me pack up Firefly, Megan?"
Megan helps Joy stuff the long balloon into a cloth
bag. Then, Elaine and Betty load the bag, basket,
and burners into the van.

"Let's go home!" Joy says.

Clutching her certificate, Megan hops into the van. With her head in the clouds, she happily leans back for the ride home.